This Little Tiger book belongs to:

_____

_____

_____

_____

For all my family
~ *M.H.*

For Dee
~ *C.W.*

LITTLE TIGER PRESS
An imprint of Magi Publications
1 The Coda Centre, 189 Munster Road,
London SW6 6AW
www.littletigerpress.com
First published in Great Britain 1995
as *Charlie and Bethan*
This edition published 2004
Text copyright © Martin Hall 1995
Illustrations copyright © Catherine Walters 1995
Martin Hall and Catherine Walters have
asserted their rights to be identified as the author
and illustrator of this work under the Copyright,
Designs and Patents Act, 1988.
A CIP catalogue record for this book
is available from the British Library
All rights reserved
ISBN 1 84506 064 4
Printed in China
2 3 4 5 6 7 8 9 10

Martin Hall

Charlie and Tess

illustrated by Catherine Walters

LITTLE TIGER PRESS

London

It was spring, and lambing time high up in the dark mountains. The weather was still cold and a blizzard was raging, so the farmer was out, tending his flock.

The farmer stopped and listened. What was that? A little plaintive, bleating cry.

It was a tiny lamb, alone and hungry.

"My, you're a small one," he said. "Can't find your mother, eh? Never mind, you come home with me."

In the farm kitchen the farmer's little daughter, Emily, made the lamb a cosy nest from a cardboard box and some old jumpers. He was very weak, but was soon hungrily sucking warm milk from a bottle with a teat on it.

"Let's call him Charlie," said Emily. Then, because they could find no ewe to look after him, Charlie became the family's own special pet, and lived with them in the farmhouse.

The farmer had a sheepdog called Tess, and as soon as Charlie was able to skip and frisk around in the farmyard, Tess was there to look after him. She made sure he did not stray too far from home, and led him back there when it was time to eat. And when Charlie was too old for the milk bottle, Tess showed him the best pastures to graze in.

All the time Charlie grew quickly. He was soon too big for the kitchen, so he slept outside in Tess's kennel. It was a tight squeeze, but the sheepdog and the lamb didn't mind. For they were friends, and kept each other warm.

They played together, when Tess was not working.
The farmer would throw a ball and watch them both
chase it. Charlie was slower than Tess, of course,
but often she would let him win.

"Sometimes I wonder if Charlie's turning into a dog,"
the farmer's wife said, as the family watched him
one day.

Charlie even had his own collar and lead. When the farmer's wife took Emily down to the village with Tess, Charlie would go as well. The people in the shops would laugh and point, as Charlie walked proudly along the road, carrying a newspaper in his mouth.

All too soon Charlie grew too big for the kennel. It was time for him to join the other sheep.

Up on the mountainside Charlie missed his adopted family. Tess was lonely as well without her friend, and cried by her kennel.

"Never mind, old girl," soothed the farmer. "We'll see Charlie soon enough when we have to move the flock to the next pasture."

That was when the trouble started. When the farmer and Tess came to move the sheep to a new field, Charlie wanted to help.

"Charlie! Go back to the other sheep," laughed the farmer. But Charlie was determined to round up the sheep with Tess, and the farmer had to push him back to the flock again.

This went on all summer, because Charlie thought he was a sheepdog.

Summer turned to autumn, and then it was
nearly winter again. Charlie sniffed the air.
It reminded him of a time long ago, when
he was lost and alone and cold. The sky
filled with clouds the colour of slate.

It grew colder and colder as the wind blew.
The sheep huddled together, but there was
little shelter. Then it began to snow.

Charlie baaed anxiously. Light snow began to
settle on his fleece. Where was Tess? Where was
the farmer? If they didn't come soon, the snow
would bury the whole flock.

At the edge of a steep slope he looked down.
He could just see the farm, but the blizzard had
already been there and covered everything.
Charlie felt very frightened indeed, for now Tess
and the farmer would not be able to reach them.

The snow blew into the sheep's eyes and
stung them with cold. Some of the weaker
ones could barely walk through the
thickening snow. Charlie knew that they
must all move down into the valley, before
it was too late.

Charlie ran ahead of the flock, but they stood stock-still, for they thought only a sheepdog could round them up. Luckily Charlie knew exactly what to do. He baaed loudly. He ran back and butted them, and pulled their fleeces with his teeth. He raced backwards and forwards, until the flock began to move, all the way down the mountainside to shelter.

Many hours later the storm died down, and a low sun shone orange across the snow-covered hills. The farmer was at last able to go out and search for his flock. He paused for a moment, looking up.

"I'm really worried – I don't know if we will be able to find them," he said to Tess. "The snow must be even deeper up there."

Tess ran on ahead. The farmer pushed on a little way and then stopped. Was that noise just the wind? He shook his head. It must have been. As he began to struggle up the mountainside, Tess started barking and tugging at his trousers with her teeth.

"What have you found, girl?" he asked.

Tess led the way down again, along a thin path through some large rocks. At the end of the path the farmer stood, amazed. All of the flock was safely gathered there, in a sheltered hollow.

"This must have been you, Charlie," he said. "You really are a sheepdog after all!"

"Woof!" Tess agreed.

"Baa," said Charlie proudly.

Great books for little heroes from Little Tiger Press

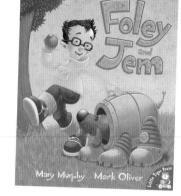

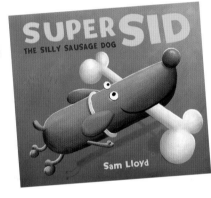

For information regarding any of the above
titles or for our catalogue, please contact us:
Little Tiger Press, 1 The Coda Centre,
189 Munster Road, London SW6 6AW
Tel: 020 7385 6333 Fax: 020 7385 7333
Email: info@littletiger.co.uk
www.littletigerpress.com